Bentley's Forever

ELIZABELLA BAKER

Gabby!

♥/Elizabella Baker

Editor: Raechelle Downing

Proofreader: Judy Zweifel, Judy's Proofreading

Cover design by: LJ, Mayhem Cover Creations

Print ISBN: 9798832099965

Library of Congress Control Number: 2018675309

Printed in the United States of America

Contents

Prologue

B entley walked into the situation room, his mind not fo- cused on work today. Ash was waiting for him at home. Their home. The one that, for the last year, they had designed, built, and turned into his sanctuary. He enjoyed coming home to her every night and, after the mess in Mexico a month ago, he knew exactly what he wanted to do. He had just started to put his plans into motion when Wes had called the team in.

"Do we know what this is all about?" he asked Arlo as he took a seat next to his team leader.

"No," Arlo simply responded. Kade, Zack, and Kyle joined them shortly later, followed by Jaime.

"I thought we were getting a few days off," Kade complained.

"So did I," Bentley responded. "Ash has a gig in Paris in a couple of days, and I planned to join her."

"Then we better make this quick," Wes boomed as he stomped through the door, Ray at his heels.

"Make what quick, boss?" Zack asked.

"Pablo Carillo," Wes spat out the name. "We have a location. We know where he will be next month and we'll be there to take his sorry ass out."

Pablo Carillo. Their Achilles' heel, or at least one of them. It all started when Leslie came back into Zack's life. They learned about how her family had helped human traffickers move girls through shipping containers. Then they met Missy, who had escaped with two little girls from one of Pablo's men. And finally, there was Jaime. Her sister was killed as a teen in Dublin when human traffickers attempted to take her. They also worked for Pablo, and for a man named King. A man whose identity they still didn't know.

It was because of Missy that they knew the identity of Pablo, but the CIA hadn't wanted to hear it when they explained the situation to Daniel. Apparently, a woman under duress wasn't enough for them. They still wanted Daniel to continue posing as a hitman so they could catch Pablo in the act and hopefully get King's identity as well. Daniel hadn't agreed, so he left the CIA and went off the grid. The team wasn't exactly sure what the man was doing these days.

"So, another trip to Mexico?" Kyle questioned.

"Actually, no," Ray spoke up. "A gala here in the States. One that I believe Ash is planning."

Everyone looked at Bentley, as if he had known that their biggest target was about to attend a gala his girlfriend was in the process of finalizing details for.

"The one for some oil tycoon?" he asked.

"The one and the same. From what I can tell, the person hosting it is a longtime friend with Pablo. It was one of many associates I flagged for interaction."

Well, I'll be damned. Coincidence or intentional? He wasn't big on coincidences, so his mind immediately went to intentional. Which meant Ash was in danger and that pissed him right off. She was his world. They had fought to be together; so much so that, at one point, he thought he had lost her to an obligation to her father. But they made it through and he would do anything to protect her.

"So, we have a month to plan," he verified.

"Yes, but we're going to need Ash's help. The last thing we want is this blowing back on her business, but it might be our only chance," Wes explained.

Bentley blew out a breath. He never thought he would see the day that his job and her business as an event planner would ever cross, but it appeared that time was here. Now he just had to explain to Ash that during one of her galas, they needed to kill a man who most likely had his own surprises up his sleeve. Yeah, the next month was about to get interesting.

Chapter 1

Bentley stared down at the solitary diamond ring sitting in the velvet box. It wasn't nearly as flashy as he felt Ash deserved but, after talking with her best friend Monica, he knew it was perfect. His girl avoided flashy except when she had to plan an event for someone. He liked to joke with her that until she met him, she was a country girl stuck in a rich girl's world and she was lucky that he came into her life to rescue her from all those expectations.

"She's going to love it." Monica's breath puffed against his outstretched hand. "I'm surprised it took you this long to finally pop the question."

He laughed at her statement. He should be offended by her blunt response, but he wasn't. She wasn't the only one who threw jabs at the fact that he hadn't yet proposed to Ash. The guys harassed him at least once a week about it, if not more. He had been the first to fall and was going to be the last one to get married at this rate. Even Kade, who just met Jaime, was already dropping hints of an upcoming wedding. Although he was pretty sure he would be able to beat Kade down the aisle.

"I told you I wanted the proposal to be perfect. Now it can be," he explained.

After returning from Mexico and watching his teammate almost lose the woman he loved because of a bad decision they, as a team, made, he finally decided to stop waiting around for the perfect moment. But then Ash told him about Paris.

She was asked to plan a "just because party," not that he had any idea what that meant, in the most beautiful place in the world, and it finally hit him. Paris was the perfect moment he'd been waiting for, and fate had been gracious enough to drop it in his lap. Ash hadn't stopped talking about how it was the one place she always loved and wanted more than anything to visit. He had been slightly surprised that with all her father's wealth and traveling, she hadn't gone yet, but he refused to look a gift horse in the mouth.

Instead, he was going to make the trip extra special for her. Just as soon as he took care of one more thing; the whole reason he was sitting in Monica's office. "Besides, I still need to speak with her father."

"You know, there's no law stating you have to ask the man." Monica all but rolled her eyes. Ash's best friend had just as much attitude and spunk as the rest of the women in his life.

But he thought about what she said and decided that wasn't true at all. At least not to him, and he knew deep down it would matter to Ash as well. Her father was the only family she had left and to have his blessing was important. Even if Bentley doubted he would give it willingly.

"My mama says otherwise and I would never go against her word," he clarified. "And you and I both know that, despite their differences, Ash would want it. She might not seek his approval as much as she used to with her day-to-day life, but for something as important as this, she would."

"You're probably right," Monica admitted, with a huff. Her face transformed from a disapproving frown to a sly smile. "What time do you meet with him, anyway? The fact that he accepted the meeting should say something," she laughed.

He wasn't sure it said anything at all, except maybe that the man wanted to tell him to his face to fuck off. They didn't exactly see eye to eye, considering he was taking Ash away from her father's business. It didn't matter that it was what she wanted. Mr. Carmichael wasn't his biggest fan, and he made it known that he didn't think Bentley was good enough. It was her father's suggestion that they meet at his office. Bentley would have preferred his home, but there was no changing the man's mind. So here he stood, about to enter the lion's den.

"In fifteen minutes, so I better get moving. I don't want to be late."

"Good luck and congrats! I'm so happy for you both!" He grinned and hugged her. One of the first things he learned about Monica was that she was a hugger, just like his sisters. It was exactly what he saw when he looked at the woman. Another little sister. Another woman he would protect with his life. Just like any of his friends' significant others or family members.

He rode the elevator up to the top floor. Like most bosses, Mr. Carmichael had a huge office at the very top of his empire. Bentley didn't even get a chance to explain who he was before the assistant stationed at the desk waved him in. Ash's father probably had a picture of his face with a giant red X across it that his assistant had memorized.

Taking a deep breath and fortifying his defenses, he stepped through the door. *I would much rather be facing down a dozen insurgents than entering this office. At least I know what to expect from them.* The first thing he noticed was the amount of flash and power the room emanated. The whole office screamed money and *I'm in charge.* Which was exactly what Bentley should have expected, considering the man's demeanor since the day they met.

"Have you finally decided to step up and make an honest woman out of my daughter?" Ash's father snidely commented without lifting his head from whatever paperwork he was working on.

Bentley's step faltered for just a second before he continued farther in the room. *See, I understand insurgents, know what to expect from them. But Ash's father, not so much.*

That wasn't exactly the welcome he envisioned, but he shouldn't be surprised. *Expect the unexpected. That's going to be my new motto.*

Pulling himself out of his musings, he confidently replied, "Yes, sir."

"Good."

One word was all the man said. Bentley continued to stare at his soon-to-be father-in-law. He looked good for his age. He knew from Ash that her father took care of himself. Not cosmetically, as his old business partner used to, but by eating right and working out. He wasn't military fit, but he wasn't the extreme either. Still not saying a word, Mr. Carmichael finally looked up.

"You're surprised I agreed." Dropping the pen, he motioned for Bentley to take a seat. Not wanting to offend, even though he would have preferred to stand, he dropped his ass into the chair. "It's no secret I think my daughter deserves better. That your line of work, or hers either for that matter, is not what I wanted for her, but I've realized something. Her happiness is all her mother ever wanted, and if that means she chooses you, then, yes, I give my blessing."

He was stunned silent, and that didn't happen often. He might not be as loud as Zack, but he wasn't as quiet as Kyle either. He was more a straight shooter. Said what was on his mind if it needed to be said. But right now he had no idea what to say other than, "Thank you, sir."

"Now I have another meeting soon, so I'm sorry to cut this short." Mr. Carmichael was effectively shooing him out the door. Bentley wouldn't complain; he got what he came for. "But one more thing before you go. I expect grandchildren and sooner rather than later. I'm not getting any younger." With that last parting shot, his soon-to-be father-in-law went back to whatever he was working on, no longer even acknowledging that Bentley was silently making his way back out of the office.

The whole way back down to the lobby, he replayed the bizarre conversation in his head, but this time, with a smile on his face. He had gone in expecting a fight. His mother had always explained that no father ever wanted to give up his daughter and expected that was true of Ash's father. But in the end, he had agreed, and now he just needed to get his ass back to Texas and plan a proposal that would knock Ash's socks off.

Chapter 2

"Wow! Just fucking wow!" Trista hooted and hollered. "First time in Paris and you're going to look amazing."

Ash's lips broke out in a huge smile. The sapphire-blue dress she had requested for her trip was absolutely perfect. Charlotte had hit it out of the park on this one. It brought out the blue in her eyes and fit her like a second skin. Bentley was going to go insane when he saw it. The man couldn't keep his hands off her to begin with, but in this one, she was about to rock his world. Bentley didn't always accompany her for work, but he was insisting this time. He wanted to be there the first time she got to experience the city of her dreams. It was the main reason she loved the man so damn much.

"I know, right?" Charlotte breathed out in amazement. "I even amazed myself with this one."

Ash chuckled at her two best friends. She had known Trista since high school, but Charlotte was new to the crew. She came with Leslie but stayed because of Zack's brother, Brooks. It was another love story she couldn't wait to watch evolve. And hopefully, plan a wedding for. Her favorite part of her business was weddings. Well, they weren't exactly jobs to her. They were fun and meant more to her than anything else. Except for Paris. That was on her bucket list.

When she received word two weeks ago that one of her new clients wanted to throw a "just for the hell of it" bash, and in Paris of all places, she jumped at the chance. She would have moved heaven and earth to make room for this party. Fortunately, she had been free, but barely. Her schedule was filling faster than she could keep up. What she really needed to do was hire an assistant, or possibly a few employees. Leslie was a saint for helping her, but that could only last for so long. Especially after her pregnant friend popped out Zack Jr. or whatever they planned to name the baby boy. Leslie had her own career to worry about.

"It's perfect," she sighed. "In every way. I can't thank you enough."

"No thanks needed." Charlotte beamed.

She couldn't keep the smile off her face. It wasn't just the dress or even the fact that in just a few days, she would be in Paris. No, it was so much more than that. It was her life altogether. Since the moment she met Bentley, everything had been a fairy tale. Not that she was a fairy-tale kind of girl, but she wanted this one to continue. Correction, she would do anything to keep it going.

"Bentley is going to flip his shit when he sees you in that." Trista whistled. Ash blushed at the compliment. She should be used to it by now. Trista was very vocal, and Bentley complimented her on the regular. He was a sweet gentleman like that. "Maybe enough that he will finally pop the question." Trista wiggled her eyebrows.

Ash merely rolled her eyes. This wasn't the first time one of their friends had mentioned something about a lack of engagement. She knew for a fact the guys took their shots every chance they got. She wished everyone would stop pestering him about it because she knew the man better than anyone, which is how she knew he was waiting for what he considered the perfect moment. He was a romantic like that. And what woman didn't swoon when the man she loved completely wanted to make everything perfect, even if it wasn't necessary?

"Oh, stop. He will when he's ready, and I don't need a ring to know he wants to spend the rest of his life with me." *I'm such a hypocrite. I insert myself into everyone else's love life like a champ.* That didn't mean she necessarily wanted people harassing Bentley. She was overprotective of her big teddy bear of a man. She mentally snorted. *Like he needs me to protect him.* "Besides, I don't see you making a move on Falcon, and we both know you've had eyes on him for months." She dragged out the last word to emphasize her point and distract Trista at the same time.

"I have NOT had eyes for him," Trista added sternly. "He's just a big burly asshole who Wes forces me to work with on occasion. We don't even like each other." Her best friend was trying way too hard to convince them.

"So have angry sex with him. That's hot as hell and you both can walk away afterward. It's a win-win," Charlotte suggested.

Ash chuckled at Charlotte's proposal, but it turned into full-out laughter when she caught Trista's stunned expression. There wasn't a lot one could say to render Trista speechless, but apparently, just the mention of sex with Falcon did it. Maybe her matchmaking wasn't over now that all the guys from Charlie Team were taken. There was a reason Charlotte had clicked so well with her and Trista.

"Even if I wanted to, he totally wouldn't go for it," Trista finally huffed out.

"Wait, does that mean you've thought about it?" Ash screeched. How did she not know that her best friend had the hots for Bravo One? The man was like a Viking brought to life. Or at least brought to the twenty-first century. If she ever needed a man to play that part, Falcon was who she would call.

"Of course, I've thought about it, okay?" Trista huffed again. "The man is a wet dream waiting to happen, but it never will. He avoids me like the plague, and on the off chance we do talk, all we do is argue. I'm pretty sure he hates my guts." Her friend actually sounded disappointed that Falcon ignored her. Trista wasn't self-centered, but no woman wanted to be ignored by the man they had feelings for.

"Or you turn him on and he doesn't want to admit it," Charlotte shrugged, but Trista didn't look convinced. She had never seen her friend look so unsure when it came to a man. Normally, Trista was unaffected. Sure, she liked to flirt and would jump into a willing man's bed, but if the man was uninterested, she would shrug it off and claim that there were a lot of other fish in the sea. So to see Trista actually fretting over Falcon was a change-up. She would certainly need to watch that particular relationship a bit more closely.

"Enough about me. This is Ash's time. She's the one going to Paris with her sexy-as-all-fuck man for a little R and R and trying to seduce him with this banging dress." Trista was deflecting, and she was going to let it happen for now.

"I don't need to seduce him," she laughed. "He already can't keep his hands off me."

"Ain't that the truth." Charlotte fanned her face and chuckled. "The first time he used that accent on me, I nearly became a puddle at his feet. Then he explained he was taken, and I instantly wanted to gouge your eyes out. At least, until I met you."

"Now you have your own sexy man to swoon over," Trista added. "And I'm over here like a spinster," her best friend whined.

"You wouldn't have to be if you just made a move," Ash mumbled under her breath before walking away.

She knew when it was time to push and when it was best to step back and wait. This was definitely a day for option number two. But she had a feeling it wouldn't stay that way for long. Trista only had so much patience and it was clearly running thin.

"Okay, now that we have the perfect dress, let me see what other stuff you created for my trip. Since you both convinced me I needed a whole new wardrobe." She rolled her eyes.

When she told her friends about the trip, they had both insisted that she couldn't possibly take any of her old outfits. She needed something fresh and new. Add in Monica's insistence that she needed a date-night outfit, hence the dress, and it would appear she was in fact getting that new wardrobe.

They spent the next hour oohing and aahing over the pieces Charlotte created and put together. Each one was better than the last and all inspired, because Trista explained exactly what she would need. Fortunately, Charlotte also knew her needs, so everything was both stylish and comfortable. That alone was reason number one she would continue recommending Charlotte to everyone who asked about a wedding dress or any wardrobe for that matter. Charlotte was a hidden gem and if they played their cards right, between Ash's event planning business and Trista's modeling friends, Charlotte would be extremely busy. She wanted that for her new friend. Charlotte deserved it after years in the shadows of another designer.

Chapter 3

He had the ring, her dad's permission, and everything was set in Paris. All that was left was to drop on one knee and ask her to marry him. Oh, and hope to hell she said yes. That part was very important. But before he could do any of that, he needed to meet with his team and figure out how they planned to take out Pablo while simultaneously not ruining his soon-to-be fiancée's business. No pressure.

"Have you told Ash yet?" He was still walking through the barn when Arlo's question stopped him in his tracks. Turning around slowly, he tossed his team leader and best friend the finger.

"No. I'm not ruining Paris for her. It's her dream place to visit and I don't need her worrying the entire time we are there," he replied matter-of-factly.

"You're making this Paris trip into a pretty big deal. Anything you care to share about it?" Arlo looked at him expectantly. Almost as if he was trying to pull the information out of Bentley's head.

"No," he grumbled, maintaining eye contact despite his urge to look away at the blatant lie. He wasn't ready to tell his team what he had planned. They liked to bust him about when he was finally going to pop the question. So, in return, he was going to make sure they were the last to know. It was the principal of the matter now. Plus, he was going to get a kick out of it when they complained, keeping them humble and all that.

"If you say so," Arlo laughed. He clearly didn't believe a word Bentley had said. "We better get going. Don't want to keep the boss waiting."

The rest of the team, including Wes, was already sitting around the large table in the situation room. He expected some type of smartass comment from his boss or one of his other teammates, but Wes just looked distracted. Not to mention extremely pissed. That couldn't be good.

With both fists on the table, Wes started, "We still don't have confirmation that Pablo is actually attending Ash's event next month. Ray is trying to get flight information, but as far as we can determine, he's not taking a commercial flight and it's a lot harder tracking a fucking personal flight."

"But the plan is to still move forward as if he is," Bentley clarified.

"Yes," Wes boomed. "Since you insist on waiting to bring Ash in until after Paris." His boss paused as if waiting for confirmation, so he nodded his head yes. "Right. So we wait and, in the meantime, see if we can get flight information. Then, when she can help, we get the guest list and hopefully information on where Pablo is staying."

"That seems like an awful lot of ifs and things needing to line up correctly," Zack commented.

"No shit, Sherlock, but it's better than what we've had in the past." The sarcasm couldn't be missed and, while it wasn't unusual for Wes, the usual humor in his tone was lacking. Any other time, he would have analyzed that a bit more, but he was too worried about his upcoming trip to give it more than a passing thought. And his boss was right. They knew Pablo's name and what he looked like, but that was all. The man seemed to move around constantly and barely left a paper trail. He stayed at expensive places but avoided credit. Ray was constantly trying to track him, but just when they thought they were getting close, Pablo would slip away. Bravo Team had been tasked with that, along with shutting down stables, but it was proving impossible to do both. They really needed him in the States for the gala so they could end things already. At least get half of the problem taken care of.

"True," Zack replied, not the least bit affected by their boss's comment.

He half-listened as they finished discussing a few other assignments that were coming up. Since technically he was off the clock in thirty minutes, he didn't need to know what was happening, so he could spend the time thinking about his upcoming plans. He was getting nervous now that shit was getting real.

He and Ash were scheduled to fly out later that day for Paris. The entire trip would take over twelve hours, which included an eight-hour overnight flight he wasn't looking forward to. He had convinced Ash to fly first class, but that didn't mean his six-foot frame would be entirely comfortable. It was why his team preferred to fly privately. The plane they owned was purposely designed for their larger frames with a hell of a lot less seating. Wes wanted comfort, not something that could be packed like sardines.

He said his goodbyes as soon as Wes stopped talking. He heard the laughs and jabs as he hauled ass out of the room, but he didn't stop long enough to verbally respond. Instead, he threw his teammates the middle finger. He preferred to get back to Ash and make sure she was ready to go. Sure enough, when he pulled up to their house barely fifteen minutes later, he found her pacing the living room.

"Is this really happening?" Ash asked as soon as he stepped foot through the threshold. "Am I really planning a party in Paris in a little over a week?" Was she nervous about planning the party or overly excited about visiting Paris? She was great at her job, so he was guessing it was the second option.

"Yes, to all the above." He walked up and wrapped her in his arms. It was the best place, and he loved the way she fit him perfectly, as if they were made for each other. Not just her made for him. No, he wasn't that type of guy and his mama would be sure to smack him silly if he was. He was all for equality, so "made for each other" was the perfect way to describe them.

"Please tell me I'm not grossly overthinking this whole thing," she panicked. Okay, so maybe it was option one. She would probably elbow him for his next comment, but sometimes honesty was just best.

With a laugh, he answered, "You are definitely overthinking things, but that's why I love you. You just want everything to be perfect and it shows. Your business is better because of it, but try to have some fun while we're there. This isn't just about work. It's the chance for us to get a little vacation in as well."

"You're right," she sighed. "I know you're right. I can't let my overthinking spoil our first trip to Paris." She shook out her body while still in his arms, as if she was physically shaking off all the negative thoughts she had carried around. "Okay, now I'm ready to go."

"That's my girl." He kissed her neck before finally releasing her. "Now where's the luggage? We best get on the road."

"In the kitchen," she replied sheepishly.

That look could only mean one thing. Sure enough, his assumption was correct. Over-packing didn't even cover the three large suitcases currently sitting next to the island, or the large garment bag draped over them. They were only going for a week and a half and he knew damn well the small stack of clothes he had pulled out only took up half of one of those. Which meant she managed to fill over two suitcases full of clothes.

"How much did you pack? It looks like enough for an entire month. If not more!"

"Charlotte created an entirely new wardrobe for me, but I wasn't sure what we would do while we were there, so I packed extras. It's not that much," she huffed.

Dropping a light peck on her lips, he shook his head as he moved to grab the bags. Her version of not that much was probably the biggest understatement he had ever heard. Nothing could be farther from the truth. Whatever happened to his simple girlfriend who didn't need much? It just showed how nervous she really was. Slapping a smile on his face, he grabbed the bags but said nothing more. This vacation meant too much to him to let a little disagreement ruin anything.

Chapter 4

Seriously, could anything else go wrong? Their first flight had to make an emergency landing, which caused them to miss their second flight, so they had to wait all night to catch a new one. Then, when she finally arrived in Paris, Ash discovered the caterer had accidentally double-booked, and since the other event was with a well-known event planner she had worked with in the past, the caterer chose that event instead. So Ash was forced to find another one on short notice.

Luckily, her client was super laid-back and didn't want anything fancy. She just liked to entertain anytime she was in her Paris home.

Now, the party was tomorrow and Ash was running around like a chicken with her head cut off; she had yet to hire an assistant and, as much as she loved Bentley, there was only so much he could do to help. The man might have grown up with three women, but an eye for design he did not have.

"Are you sure there isn't anything I can help with?" Bentley's voice was laced with concern. Probably because she had spent the last five days panicking rather than enjoying the city like she originally planned. Oh, she still got to see the sights, but all of her carefully planned days went up in smoke. She would have cried if it weren't so funny. Not like haha funny, but more like the universe was telling her to calm the fuck down and just enjoy what she had rather than aiming for perfection. Since that was a character flaw she already knew she had, she really wanted to throw the universe the middle finger.

"No, I'm good. I guess it's time I stop talking about hiring an assistant and actually do it. I'm going to ask Trista the moment we get back if she has anyone at any of the shelters who might be interested. If not, I'll put an ad out. No more procrastination," she finished with determination.

"That's the spirit. If you don't happen to find someone through Trista, please promise me that Ray or even Arlo does a background check on any of the applicants. I don't want anyone that close to you unless they've been fully vetted."

Ash wanted desperately to roll her eyes at the remark, but he wouldn't appreciate it, and he only had her best interest at heart. Considering who he worked for and what he did for a living, she fully understood his need to protect her.

"I promise." She smiled. Standing up on her toes, she planted a big, juicy kiss on his lips. One that he deepened until she was out of breath and panting for more. "Damn, that wasn't fair," she whined. "We need to meet my client downstairs in ten minutes."

"Let's just call it a teaser for later. I'm thinking you earned a nice massage before your big party tomorrow." He winked and laughed. And now she was going to need to change her panties before the meeting. Damn that man and his sexy wink. He was going to be the death of her. It would be an orgasmic and sex-fulfilled death, but dead nonetheless. With a sigh, she quickly grabbed a change of outfit. Thank goodness she had over-packed; she had enough clothes to change her outfits ten times over.

Her meeting with her client didn't last nearly as long as she expected. Mara was completely satisfied with everything she had set up and, since she was a professional, she never once let on to the fact that, behind the scenes, she looked like a madman, finalizing the last of the details.

This wasn't the first time she had met Mara. She originally met her during a party she threw for another client. Mara hadn't stopped talking about how much she loved Ash's work and that she needed an excuse to hire her. Apparently, a "just because" party was the perfect excuse.

This would normally be where someone would joke about how the other half lives, but considering until she met Bentley, she was literally living that life, she wouldn't comment. The difference was that, now, she recognized the importance of being humble, and not like those people she grew up around; the life her father insisted she stay in and the one he still to this day followed like a bible. Image was the only thing that mattered to him. He would throw those random parties just because he felt it was expected of him to impress friends that weren't really friends. Meeting Bentley and his team was a real eye-opener.

It also made her one hell of a better event planner. Plus, she managed to get some really great new friends out of the deal. Real friends. Not the fake kind her father expected.

The next forty-eight hours flew by. As promised, she got her massage, but with a little something extra. The party went off without a hitch despite all the problems before it even started. Mara was happy, and that's all that mattered; another satisfied client to add to her portfolio. Now, she was getting fancied up in that killer dress Charlotte made for her. Bentley refused to tell her where they were going or what they were doing to celebrate. It was his way of teaching her patience, or at least, that's what he always told her every damn time he wanted something to be a surprise. One would think she would be getting used to it, but that would be a lie. She was as impatient as she was the first time he did it to her.

"Are you . . ." she heard Bentley start to say, but when she caught his eye in the mirror, he had stopped dead in his tracks. His eyes were roaming over every inch of her body. And she liked the look she saw on his face.

"Wow, you look amazing." His lust-filled gaze finally reached hers.

"I'm ready, if that's what you came in here to ask." She smiled.

Turning around, she did her own scan. He wasn't wearing a tuxedo like the first time they got dressed up, but he wasn't any less drool-worthy in his dress pants and a button-down shirt. There was something to be said about a man who could easily wear tactile gear one minute and a suit the next. And luckily for her, he was all hers.

Stepping in front of him, she whispered, "You look pretty amazing yourself."

With lightning-fast reflexes, Bentley wrapped his arm around her waist and dipped her for a kiss, effectively nibbling off her carefully placed lipstick. She could tell the moment he realized she wasn't wearing any panties because his hands stilled and she felt the air he sucked in with the giant breath he took.

"Care to explain why you aren't wearing anything under this dress?" he growled against her mouth.

She was playing with fire, but instead of backing away, she was jumping in headfirst. "The dress doesn't exactly allow for them," she purred.

"Damn, you're killin' me," he groaned. "I reckon we better leave before I lose all good sense."

He lifted her up and moved away slowly, but it took her several moments to convince her body to move. His Southern drawl came on thick when he was turned on and right now it was in full swing. She was tempted to tell him to hell with their plans and they could stay in, but the stubborn set of his jaw warned he wouldn't be swayed. Instead, she sucked it up and let him take her hand. Maybe if she thought about something other than how good he looked, her need to climb him like a tree would go away. *Probably not.*

A town car awaited them when they stepped outside the hotel, and nearly thirty minutes later, they pulled up to a dock that she recognized as boarding for a dinner cruise on the Seine River. She had always wanted to see the sights while she traveled along the river.

"How did you know?" She breathed out in awe. She'd never told anyone, but it didn't surprise her that Bentley had known. Some days, it seemed like the man could read her mind. He was so in tune with her thoughts and feelings.

"I just know you." Bentley placed a soft kiss on her temple before following the host to their table.

While the boat wasn't large, she expected there to be more tables and diners, but looking around, she noted they had the place to themselves. With one raised eyebrow, she silently questioned Bentley.

"I wanted the boat to ourselves." He shrugged nonchalantly.

But instead of it having the effect he was probably aiming for, her heart began to thump wildly in her chest. Bentley was always a romantic and never missed an opportunity to make something special for her, but he was also frugal to a fault. Having grown up with very little, he rarely splurged. Which could only mean one thing. She sucked in a breath as the server silently poured them each some water and a glass of champagne.

She waited until the server was finished and walked away before she finally blurted out, eyes wide, "Oh my God! You're going to propose, aren't you?"

Bentley simply chuckled when she clasped a hand over her mouth. She hadn't realized she had said her thoughts out loud.

"Your lack of a filter and impatience for surprises is just two of the many reasons I love you so much." She watched as he reached into his pocket and pulled out a box. Dropping to one knee, he continued to laugh as he said, "I was planning to wait until dessert to ask, but since you already guessed..."

He gave her a dramatic pause and a shake of the head that, any other time, would have caused her to roll her eyes. But her eyes were too fixated on the box in his hand and the fact that he was giving her one of his panty-melting smiles. She couldn't think clearly enough to roll them.

"Ash, my love. Will you do me the honor of becoming my wife?"

"Yes! A million times, yes!" she squealed. He slid the solitary diamond ring on her finger, then she threw herself at him as he wrapped her in a hug and spun around. Burying her head in his neck, she took in the scent that was so uniquely him. She hadn't thought she could love Bentley more than she already did, but having him propose to her in Paris made her realize how lucky she really was. Lucky to have the love of such an amazing man.

Chapter 5

In typical Ash fashion, she had taken his carefully planned proposal and thrown it out the window. He hadn't lied to her when he said it was one of the many reasons he loved her. He would never stifle her personality so, as usual, he rolled with the punches and dropped to one knee, confirming that he did in fact plan to propose to her.

They spent the rest of the dinner cruise laughing about her outburst, enjoying good food, and appreciating the sights. But he was more than eager to get back to the hotel and begin celebrating in private with his new fiancée. He would never get tired of that word. At least, not until he could change it to wife which, according to Ash, would be sooner rather than later. As expected, she didn't want a long engagement or a big wedding. She had made it very clear after dinner that she just wanted to be his as soon as she could get everything put together. Placing his hand on her lower back, he escorted her off the boat and was

suddenly reminded of their conversation before they left the roo
m.

"I'm going to enjoy getting you out of this dress just as soon
as we get into the room," he growled into her ear.

The shiver that coursed through her body only fueled him
on. He would never tire of her. Her body called to him on a
primitive level, making the thirty-minute drive back pure torture. Unlike the first time they attended a formal event together,
this town car didn't have a privacy shield, so there was no way
he could start anything yet, despite how much he wanted to.
Instead, he teased her with kisses along her neck, whispering all
the things he was going to do to her just as soon as they arrived.

By the time they stepped foot into the hotel lobby, he was
supporting one hell of an uncomfortable erection, and Ash had
a pretty blush spreading down her throat and across her chest.
He should feel bad that they were walking through the fancy
lobby like horny teenagers, but he really didn't. All he could
think about was the fact that his fiancée had nothing beneath
that dress.

The elevator doors barely clicked shut before he backed her
into the corner and crashed his lips to hers. "You knew it would
drive me crazy knowing you had nothing on beneath this," he
whispered as he nibbled on her ear.

"That was the plan," she panted with her head thrown back,
giving him better access to her ear and neck.

"Well, it worked."

He ran his hands up the outsides of her thighs as he pressed
his erection into her belly. In heels, she was only a few inches
shorter than him, so it wouldn't take more than a little lift to

have her straddling him. But the sound of them reaching their floor was enough to have him pulling away. With their fingers entwined, he all but dragged her towards their room, both of them giggling as he threw open the door. Slamming it with his foot, he had her spun around with her back against the wall before she could even catch her breath.

"I need you now." His lips met hers. Lifting the dress, he picked her up so she could wrap her legs around him. He leaned in and ground his erection against her bare crotch.

"You still have too many clothes on," Ash grumbled as she pulled his shirt from his dress pants. As much as he wanted to take her against the wall, he forced himself to slow things down. Pushing off the wall, he never stopped kissing her as he made the few steps to the bed.

Setting her down on the floor, he raked his eyes up her long legs, lean body, and finally met her beautiful honey-brown eyes. "It's like unwrapping the best present in the world." He held her lust-filled eyes as he slowly unzipped the dress down her side. Not only did the dress not allow for panties, but it also didn't need a bra; within seconds, the dress was pooling around her ankles, leaving her naked. Taking her hand, he helped her step out of the dress, but stopped her as she leaned down to take off the shoes.

"Those are stayin' on this evenin'." His voice was definitely huskier than usual.

"Yes, sir." His saucy-mouthed fiancée had the audacity to wink.

No longer caring to take his time, he ripped his shirt, sending the buttons flying, and quickly pulled the undershirt over his head. Ash continued to watch him through her lashes as he hastily got rid of the rest of his clothing.

"Turn around and bend over," he demanded. "I want to see your legs in those heels as I take you from behind." He watched the blush creep up her cheeks just before she spun around.

With her legs spread slightly apart, he took a moment to just worship her perfect heart-shaped ass. She continued to do yoga, and he thanked the good lord each day that she did. Dropping to his knees, he palmed her cheeks as he pulled her away from the bed to lick her already drenched lips. Her groan spurred him on as he continued to flick her clit with his tongue. He was determined to pull her first orgasm of the night out with just his tongue. Lapping her up like the starved man he was, he bit her nub again when he knew she was close. Screaming his name, she came on his tongue as he fisted his cock and slammed into her drenched core, not giving her any time to come down.

"Fuck yes." Her moan was suppressed by the comforter as he watched her dig her fingers in next to her head. Seeing her ring shine, he laced his own fingers with hers and squeezed. *Mine.* That one little ring meant she was his forever.

His free hand trailed lazily up her belly as he continued to drive into her. Each time he reached her nipple, he would pinch the bud, releasing more moans from her before trailing his hand back down and playing with her clit. He continued the trail back and forth as he pumped into her, not letting her get used to one sensation before he switched it up. It was his way of torturing her for the no panties he was forced to think about all evening.

"Bentley, please." She twisted her head to find his eyes as she begged. He knew exactly what she wanted, but he loved to hear her say it.

"Please what, my love?" he ground out. He was holding back himself, just waiting for her to finish. "What do you need?"

"Please..." she moaned as she shoved his hand down to her clit, telling him without words exactly what she needed. Unable to wait any longer, he rubbed until he could feel her walls quake and they both finished together. Their combined juices slid down her leg. With their hands still locked together, he collapsed on top of her for just a few moments. Once he had his breathing under control, he slipped out of her wet heat. He could hear a whimper escape her lips and he rolled her over.

"Let's shower and clean up. I feel like taking care of my fiancée tonight," he whispered in her ear before leading her to the bathroom. Cranking the water on, he slipped his arms around her waist from behind as he waited for it to heat up.

"Are you happy?" he asked as he nibbled on her ear. He wasn't an insecure man, but he had made it his life mission to make sure she was always happy, so every so often he made sure to ask. He figured tonight was one of those times.

"Deliriously happy." She looked up and met his eyes in the mirror. He could look into her honey-brown eyes every day and never get tired of them. Giving her a small smile in return, he pulled her underneath the pulsing jets.

He meant it when he told her he wanted to take care of her, so he took his time scrubbing every inch of her body; some places more than others because damn, he would never get tired of her ass or nipples. By the time he was done, he was more than ready for another round.

After towel drying them both off, he carried her back to the bed and laid her down, loving the way her blonde hair fanned out on the pillow. Her come-hither look brought a smile to his face as he trailed kisses along her jaw and lips. Cradling himself between her legs, he slowly entered her and proceeded to make love to his fiancée, the love of his life.

Chapter 6

They were back from Paris. Things had gone better than expected, at least from his point of view, but now it was time for reality. He was holding Ash's hand, playing with her engagement ring as they drove to the barn. His fiancée had only slightly questioned why he wanted her to join him at work. While he hadn't completely lied when he explained that Wes needed her help with their next assignment, he also didn't exactly tell her all of it. He had no idea how she was going to handle the fact that they wanted to capture and eventually kill a guest at one of her events. *This is going to be the shortest engagement in the history of engagements.*

"Do you think Wes is ever going to find someone, or is he always going to be this grumpy?" Ash's question jarred him out of his thoughts. Her relationship meddling knew no bounds. He simply chuckled before answering her.

"That's one person's love life you are going to want to stay far away from."

"Oh, come on. You can't tell me you wouldn't love to give back just a little of the harassment he dishes out."

Of course he would, but the sad reality was he doubted his boss would ever settle down. There was something about the man that just screamed stay away. However, this is one time he would be thrilled if he was wrong.

"Even if he ever found someone, I highly doubt he would bring her around until he was absolutely sure it was a forever thing. Wes doesn't do casual."

Not once, in all the years he worked for Wes, did he ever talk about a woman or hooking up or any of those things. For all he knew, the damn man was a monk or celibate or whatever the word would be.

"Well, I really hope he finds a forever thing." She gave him a wide smile.

"Because you like to matchmaker or because you're feeling extra romantic with my ring on your finger?" he laughed. They had come back from Paris three days ago and he still caught her glancing at it with loving eyes. If that didn't make his heart swell, then he didn't know what would. She was truly happy, and that was all he ever wanted. Which was why he had postponed this conversation a few days, despite Wes's demands. He just couldn't bear to see that happy smile disappear so soon.

"Maybe a little bit of both," she laughed right along with him.

They got to the barn sooner than he hoped and walked in together, hand in hand. They had already made the announcement through texts and calls. There hadn't been a shortage of congratulations. Everyone was finally happy that he had popped the question, so he was fully prepared for the response he got the moment they stepped into the situation room.

"Well, well, well. Look who finally decided to officially take Ash off the market," Zack joked.

"She was always off the market, dickhead," he tossed back.

"I don't know, man," Zack continued. "I think until she has your last name, she's still a free agent." Zack laughed, but he was the only one.

Both Kyle and Kade threw him a dirty look; neither had popped the question yet nor gone down the aisle. Besides their team leader, Zack was the only one married. But that man had been so damn possessive about Leslie, he made it clear that he would marry and knock her up as soon as possible. Both of which he did.

"Are we done talking about everyone's love life, or do you still need time?" Wes sarcastically asked the group.

"Actually, since you asked," Ash started, but Wes cut her off before she could continue.

"That was rhetorical and don't start your shit before I take back every nice thing I said about you the last few days."

Bentley's fiancée huffed and mumbled something about stubborn-ass man under her breath. He wondered if she even realized she sounded exactly like Wes every time he complained about the women of the group.

"Now let's get down to business," Wes boomed. "Ash, I'm assuming that man of yours didn't explain everything, otherwise you would be bitching at me a hell of a lot more."

He tossed his boss a dirty look, one Wes simply brushed off and didn't even acknowledge. Whatever happened to having his back and being part of the team? Wes must really be in a bad mood.

"What does he mean by 'everything'?" Ash was no longer holding his hand but instead facing him with her hands on her hips and a scowl on her face. Pretty much exactly what he figured she would look like when she found out. Better to just rip off the Band-Aid.

"Remember Pablo Carillo?"

"The human trafficking guy that you guys have been looking for?" She looked a little less pissed.

"That would be the one," he began to explain. "We believe he will be at the event you're planning for in two weeks. The gala for that oil tycoon." He could never remember all of her clients' names. He had it set up that Ray would run background checks every time she spoke to someone new, but at this point, Ash just sent him information directly. He only learned about her events when she talked about her day.

"So, what's your plan? To kill him during the gala?" She looked to each and every one of them. When no one denied it or laughed at how outrageous her suggestion was, her look went from surprised to dangerously pissed. "Absolutely fucking not. I have a reputation to uphold, and having a guest die during my event isn't exactly going to make people want to hire me!" she screamed.

"We weren't necessarily thinking during the gala, but more like exploring our options once we confirmed he was in town," Arlo added.

"You, of all people, should know the risks. Leah is the one catering the event and I can't see her being thrilled with this idea either," Ash huffed. It was Arlo's lack of a response that had Ash leaning forward. "Wait, you haven't told her yet, have you?"

"We wanted to talk to you about it first," Arlo tried to placate Ash, but it was clear his fiancée wasn't having any of it. "We first need confirmation he's attending before we make a decision. It's the reason we're only telling you."

Now Ash plopped herself into a chair and just looked at him. He wasn't sure if it was a plea for help or her contemplating how to murder a room full of former military men. If anyone would be able to pull it off, it was her. Although she could probably wrangle in the rest of the group of ladies. Jaime was a hothead, so she would gladly join. Leah would if Ash explained why. Leslie was far enough in her pregnancy that she was bound to be contemplating Zack's murder at least a couple of times a day. The only one who would be on the fence was Missy. She was too sweet to kill any of them, and he doubted Kyle would have given her any reason to do so.

"So, basically, either way, this guy's murder is going to be tied to the gala."

It wasn't a question and none of them bothered to answer as such. However, to drive the point home, Wes added, "It might be the only time we know his location. He moves around too much in Mexico and Bravo Team is too busy to try to watch his every move. The only other option would be to send Charlie Team and who knows how long that would take. This is easier and faster."

That was probably the only thing Wes could have said that would convince Ash. She never wanted Bentley to be gone for more than a couple of days, and now that his teammates were all settled down and starting to have families, Wes tried to keep all of their assignments to less than a week, unless it was absolutely necessary. The women understood because they knew Wes did it as a last resort.

"Okay, what do you need from me?" she sighed.

"Is the host having you set up rooms or allowing you access to the guest list?" Arlo asked.

"His wife is who I work with mostly. But to answer your questions, yes to both."

"So, what we need is to see that guest list and try to get as much information as we can about where he will be staying, and with whom," Wes replied.

"I'll get you as much information as I can."

She no longer sounded mad, and she was once again holding Bentley's hand under the table. It put his mind at ease. No matter what they dealt with, they would always come out of it stronger and together. She was his other half, after all. They spent another hour going over a few more details, but they couldn't put anything into motion until they had more information. And the best part was that he would be by her side throughout it all because there was no way he was letting his job bring her any harm.

Chapter 7

There were less than five days left until the event, and even though she was able to confirm that Pablo Carillo would in fact be attending with his wife, she had no idea where he would be staying. Her client's husband was keeping that one close to the vest. Having made the arrangements himself, the team was trying to figure out another way to obtain the information. A huge part of her really hoped they succeeded because from everything Bentley had told her, the man was truly awful. But there was still that small part that really wished they could accomplish their goal without it having to touch her gala. Her business was still growing, so she couldn't afford a black stain on it, and death was a huge black stain. But she needed to trust that Bentley wouldn't do anything to hurt her or her business. He was her biggest supporter.

Speak of the devil. She leaned back into his broad chest as he wrapped his arms around her middle.

"Why the frown?" he whispered next to her ear before placing a kiss on her neck. She sighed with each kiss he placed.

"How did you know I was frowning?" He had come up behind her, so he couldn't see her face.

"I could tell by the way you were standing," he chuckled. "That, and you put your nail in your mouth when you frown."

She dropped the opposing hand. She didn't bite her nails anymore, or even pick at them, but Bentley was right. Any time she was stressed or, as he said, frowning, she would put the nail in her mouth as if it would help her solve all of her problems.

"I'm worried," she admitted.

Spinning her around to look into her eyes, he tipped her chin up until she was getting lost in his baby blues. "I know you are, but trust that I'll make sure everything works out. I love you too much to let anything go wrong."

That made her smile and eased her fear just a bit. She had just been thinking about how she needed to trust him and here he was reassuring her.

"Not that I don't want to talk about work, but have you thought any more on when you wanted to get married? I know I just asked, but I guess I was just curious how long you were going to make me wait."

He gave her a lopsided smile that still made her swoon after all this time. She had plans to torture him and say she wanted a super long engagement, but she couldn't bring herself to cause what she was sure would be a frown on his handsome face, so instead, she told him exactly what she had planned.

"I was actually thinking of a really short engagement. How does six weeks from now sound? I checked with Charlotte and she can get a dress made for me in enough time and, besides my father, everyone else will be thrilled. Especially your mother and sisters who practically begged me not to wait too long," she laughed.

The one thing she hadn't expected when she met Bentley was to gain a mother and two sisters in the process. They might not live in the same state, but they spoke several times a week, and got along better than she ever expected. It probably had to do with the fact that Bentley's family was down to earth and liked life to be drama-free. It was the exact opposite of what she grew up with and exactly what she craved her entire life.

"It sounds perfect. I can't wait to tell the guys." Bentley had a huge smile on his face. "Just family and friends?"

"Oh my God, yes," she sighed drastically. "I don't care what my father says, I'm not inviting anyone from my old life except Trista and Monica. As far as I'm concerned, they are the only ones who matter to me, and truthfully, I haven't even spoken to anyone else. No way in hell will anyone else from my past be coming to our wedding. Especially not any of my father's fancy friends." That last part, she couldn't hide the disdain in her voice. Friends was a loose term to describe the people her father associated with.

"I love when you speak your mind."

She knew he meant that. He had fought so hard when they first met to get her to do the things that made her happy. She had almost thrown it all away because of some stupid obligation she thought she owed her father. Fortunately, she had two best friends who were more than happy to set her straight. Not once had she regretted her decision to move to Texas to be with Bentley and start her new business. A business that was booming if she stopped and thought about it. She was building a kick-ass brand with her own personal vendors. Leah was catering and now Charlotte was willing to design dresses. If she played her cards right, she would have every vendor she needed on her te am.

"Thank you for always supporting my dreams and going along with my crazy, hairbrained ideas."

She tried to be serious but ended up laughing when he nodded in agreement at the crazy part. Her business was successful because she didn't just sit back and play it safe. She went after what she wanted, even if that meant taking jobs from people no one else would because they were too difficult. She absolutely loved the challenge and was happy that she finally convinced Leah to cater.

"I promised I would never let you give up on your dreams." He shrugged nonchalantly. "I'm just keeping my promise." His modesty was one of the many reasons she fell in love with him. He wasn't a showboat. He didn't need the praise or ego boost. He was just the right amount of comfortable with himself and didn't realize how downright sexy he looked. And he was about to be hers for the rest of his life. She was one lucky-ass woman.

"And I love you for that." She smiled. "But we still need to figure out how we plan to get Pablo alone, and you *know* not to kill him at my gala." She laughed, but they both knew it was fake. She was too damn nervous to give it her usual sassy remark.

"Everything will work out. I promise."

He kissed her forehead and the universe must have heard his words because seconds later her phone was ringing and she recognized it as her client for the gala. Giving Bentley the "one moment" finger, she stepped away to take the call.

"Dreams Do Come True Event Planning. Ash speaking."

When it had come time to pick a name for her company, she had thought it would take her forever to decide, but one night as she and Bentley were cuddling, he mentioned that dreams really could come true. Like a lightbulb had gone off, her business name was picked and the next day she had started the paperwork to make it official. It was more true now than ever.

"Hello, Ash. This is Mrs. DeAngelo. I had a last-minute request that I was hoping you could fulfill. I know my husband *claims* he has the transportation completely taken care of, but we have one guest who is staying at our country home outside of the city. As you know, the rest of the out-of-town guests will be staying at the hotel, but one of his childhood friends is coming in and using our second home. Any chance you can arrange a car service to and from the gala the day of?"

Would it be bad to do a little jig? Or sound too eager? Pulling every ounce of professionalism she had in her body, she calmly answered, "Absolutely, Mrs. DeAngelo. Just send me the address and I can get it all set up for you."

"Oh, thank you so much, Ash! You have made this a seamless experience. I can't stop bragging to my friends about what a great job you've done so far. I'll talk to you again soon. Bye-bye."

The whole conversation only took a matter of moments, but it was exactly the break she needed. "Bentley," she screamed with excitement. He must not have gone far because three seconds after she yelled his name, he came around the corner with one eyebrow raised. "You won't believe who that was."

"Mrs. DeAngelo," he replied with a smirk. When she tossed him a look like he just kicked her puppy, he immediately explained. "I might have been eavesdropping just a bit."

"I know damn well your mama raised you better than that," she chided. "We'll come back to that, but yes, you're correct, and I think we just got the information we need. She's requesting a car service for her husband's childhood friend who will be staying at their country home outside the city."

Now it was Bentley who looked excited. "Now that we know where he might be staying, we can put a plan into motion. Let me call Wes. Even if she changes her mind, Ray can find the address," he smiled. "I told you it would all work out."

She really hoped so. For the first time since Wes spoke to her about Pablo Carillo and how he needed her help because the man was attending the gala, she actually felt like things might turn out okay. Not only that, but something Mrs. DeAngelo said really resonated with her.

Her client was using word of mouth to help spread her name. That was the best compliment she could have ever received. As long as she never found out Ash assisted with killing one of her guests, that is, but that was a problem for another day. Right now, she was too happy with the call to let a minor detail ruin it. Her dreams really were coming true, one at a time. And the final one would come in just six weeks when she finally married her savior.

Chapter 8

Ash's information turned out to be invaluable. They staked out the DeAngelo country home until Pablo arrived two days before the party. After much consideration, they decided to watch the situation closely but move after the gala. While they preferred to finish it quicker, none of them wanted to ruin the event. So here they were, the day after the gala, and Pablo was still in town and with a routine they were able to identify.

"Charlie Three and Four in position," Zack radioed over the mic. Both snipers were set up in a tree about five hundred feet from their current location. From what they could tell, Pablo didn't come with any of his guards and it was only him and his wife. He couldn't tell if it was because the man was cocky or just dumb. Either way, it worked in their favor.

"Charlie Five in position," Kyle's voice came over next. He and Blitz were positioned on the opposite side of them. If Pablo decided to run, Kyle would send Blitz after him.

Which left Bentley, Arlo, and Wes to actually confront Pablo just inside the woods. Right on schedule, Pablo exited the back of the house and started walking their way. The man stepped just far enough to be covered by the trees when they finally decided to move out from their current positions.

"Pablo Carillo," Wes growled.

"Well, if it isn't Mr. Westley James. I should have known coming to the States was a bad idea, but King assured me it would be fine. Looks like even he can't see the future."

Pablo's arrogance couldn't be ignored. For a man who was about to die, and Bentley was pretty sure Pablo knew that, the man was still an arrogant ass.

"And who is King?" Wes looked calm.

To an outsider like Pablo, it would seem like Wes lacked emotion, but the way his boss's eyes squinted just a bit more, plus the tic in his jaw said it all. Instead of being happy that they were about to eliminate a huge foe, Wes was pissed.

"You'll know when King wants you to know."

It was an arrogant answer. He would love nothing more than to just shoot the asshole, but they needed answers. They had gotten lucky when they realized that each night Pablo went out for a walk alone. It was a stupid rookie mistake. One they could only assume he made because he was used to doing something similar back home.

"How does a man, or maybe a woman, attract so many people willing to sacrifice themselves to keep their identity a secret?" Wes asked.

It baffled both teams that they couldn't even figure out the gender of King. Everyone just referred to the person by the name but never by any type of identifiable characteristic. And then there was the fact that Hector, one of King's henchmen, killed himself rather than be questioned. The entire situation was becoming more and more bizarre. Normally, they had some inkling of a person they were tracking, but not this time.

"Loyalty." Pablo gave a simple one-word answer before pulling a gun from his pocket and firing at Wes.

They had prepared for a firefight, so they returned fire but aimed for non-kill shots because they were hoping to question him more. Pablo took two shots to the shoulder and one to the thigh but still managed to continue shooting, as if he had human strength; at least one of those shots should have slowed him down, but he continued to let off shots one after another.

A bullet whizzing by Bentley's ear caught his attention. All of the shots Pablo had let off before that had hit off the dirt or gone completely out of the way, but that last one was more accurate and too close to home. He was ready to end things when he watched Pablo's head explode in front of his eyes.

"Target neutralized," Kade called over the mic.

He, Arlo, and Wes walked over to where the body lay crumpled on the ground. The top of Pablo's head was taken clean off. There was no way the man survived that one.

"Son of a bitch," Wes grumbled under his breath.

"There was no choice. He wasn't giving up until we killed him. Pretty sure that was the plan the moment he recognized you," Arlo added.

"I know, damn it. I was just hoping for a different outcome," Wes snapped. His boss's temper was short lately. As in, almost nonexistent. "Check the body and then we'll move out. I'll call my contact and get this mess cleaned up."

He quickly checked the man's pockets but found nothing besides the gun and a phone. Since they had no reason to take either, they left everything and silently moved back out of the forest to their SUVs.

It turned out to be a better night than he thought. Pablo was dead and no one from his team was hurt in the process. The only downside was they didn't have any new information on King. He was beginning to wonder if they ever would. The person knew how to keep their identity hidden, that was clear.

Chapter 9

Ash wasn't exactly sure what she had expected, but she was relieved that Mrs. DeAngelo and her husband didn't blame her for the death of their friend. Wes's friend was able to make magic happen and the official police report stated a mugging gone bad. Especially since Pablo was found in the woods for one of his many nightly walks. Pablo's wife had told the police that she had begged him not to go every night, but he had insisted. So it was a win-win for everyone. Her business was still a success, and Bentley and his team were able to take out one of the bad guys. What more could she want?

"So now that we no longer have to worry about people dying at our events," Leah broke up her thoughts with a huff, "are you ready to tell me what you want me to make for your wedding? Five weeks isn't exactly that long."

"I've already told you, it's low-key. I want you to enjoy yourself just as much as the rest of us." She let out a chuckle.

Just because she planned weddings for a living didn't mean she expected hers to be anything as grand. Hell, if she didn't think her father and Bentley's mother would be unhappy, she probably would have suggested they run away and elope. But that wasn't an option, so she was doing the next best thing; their weekly Sunday barbeque, but with nicer attire. At least, that's what she was pushing for. To hell with what everyone else thought. She was the bride, and if she wanted to have a stress-free wedding, then that's exactly what she would plan. She knew she wasn't meant for the fancy parties of her old life.

"Yeah, I get that you want low-key, but I doubt burgers and hot dogs are what people are expecting." Her friend attempted to give her a stern look, but Ash knew better. Leah didn't have a mean bone in her body and she certainly didn't have the intimidation look down.

"You know damn well Bentley would be all for Terry's burgers," she replied seriously. Her soon-to-be husband had a weak spot for them. Actually, weak spot wasn't the right word. More like obsessed with them; before they started dating, it was his main food consumption. "So don't even try to say that shouldn't be a consideration," she laughed.

"You're right, and I could probably make that work." Leah waved her off. "Never mind, I'll take care of it. I know by now what everyone likes to eat and the only guests are our usual group plus your father and Bentley's family. I doubt it will be hard to please Bentley's family."

Leah didn't have to say the next part for Ash to know exactly what her friend was thinking. Her father would be hard to please, but he was the only one, and truth be told, he would just need to accept what was happening. It was as if the man had a sixth sense because her phone began to ring with a call from him.

Shoring up her walls, she took a deep breath before answering. "Hello, Father."

"Really, Ashlynn? A backyard barbeque for a wedding? That's the best you can come up with?"

No hello.

No congratulations.

No, can I help with things.

Not even a how are you.

This was exactly why she needed to brace herself before answering the phone. Her father was so damn predictable it was ridiculous.

"I'm great. Thank you for asking," she sarcastically replied instead.

"Now's not the time for childish behavior, Ashlynn," her father chided. "This is a serious discussion."

The fact that he continued to use her full name, plus his blatant disrespect for her wishes, was enough for her to continue with the so-called childish behavior.

"And what discussion might that be?"

She was fully aware Leah could hear everything that was being said, despite her friend's attempt to look anywhere but at her. This wasn't the first time Leah had been present during a conversation with her father. They usually all ended the same.

"Your wedding, Ashlynn." She could hear the clear frustration through the phone. "You know, the once-in-a-lifetime event that is supposed to be magical. Not just some barnyard rodeo."

"It's *my* wedding. Which means I can have whatever I want and it will be magical because it's mine."

Why was she even having to explain herself? *Oh yeah, because this is my father and nothing is ever good enough.*

"Honey, if you're just doing this because of Bentley and what he expects, or it's only what he can afford, I assure you I will pay for whatever dream wedding you want." Her father was practically pleading with her, but she was too pissed to care. How dare he insinuate such nonsense.

"First of all, *Father*, money was never the motivation behind any decision being made when it came to my wedding. Second of all, despite what you think, Bentley and I do very well for ourselves. Not that it's any of your business. I can assure you if I wanted a big extravagant wedding, that's exactly what Bentley would give me. No matter what it cost because he loves me and wants me to be happy. And lastly, every decision about the wedding so far has been my idea. Bentley is leaving it up to me, and I'm doing exactly what I want. Stress-free and laid-back. I want to enjoy the day. So, to answer your original question, yes. Yes, I'm really having a backyard barbeque for my wedding."

She was out of breath by the time she was done with her little rant, and from the corner of her eye, she could see Leah's bulging stare. While she was no longer meek, like she used to be, it was rare for her to unleash on her father like that. But she refused to apologize. She wasn't wrong. He was.

"Fine, have it your way." There was no goodbye before her father hung up on her. Not that she expected one. Why would there be a goodbye when she never even got a hello.

"I take it your father isn't happy about your plans for the wedding," Leah commented quietly.

"That's the understatement of the year," she huffed out. "I expected it, but just hearing him comment that Bentley can't take care of me financially really pushed me over the edge. Why does everything have to be about money with him."

She rubbed the necklace under her sweater. It had been her mother's, and she wore it every day. She wished her mother was still alive. She would have understood her need for a more intimate wedding. Even though her mother died when she was eight, she could still remember her mother always encouraging her to follow her heart and do what made her happy. She wished her father would remember those times. The only thing he ever remembered was the deathbed promise he made. To take care of her no matter what. Unfortunately, what her mother meant and how her father interpreted it were two completely different things.

"From what you've told me and what I've heard from your conversations," Leah chuckled, "I really think that your father truly believes the only way to take care of someone is by having money."

Leah was right. She always knew that. She just hoped after all this time, he would realize that his daughter was doing fine and just be happy for her. That was probably way too much to ask at this point in their life.

"Well, since he's going to be mad at me no matter what I do, I might as well go all out and serve Terry's burgers."

Leah chuckled as she shook her head. Her friend probably thought she was crazy, and maybe she was, but social norms be damned. She was doing things her way and Bentley was going to love having his favorite food served. At the end of the day, that's all that mattered.

Chapter 10

S hit, he was running late. He was supposed to be home an hour ago. His mother and two sisters were set to arrive any minute, and he hated being rushed, but the stupid client he was working with didn't seem to think time existed. A typical rich boy who wanted to look good in front of his friends, so he hired a bodyguard for a luncheon. It was ridiculous and pointless, but Wes charged an extreme amount, and the idiot father was more than willing to pay, so who was he to complain about easy money and an even easier gig? And any other time he wouldn't have, but right now it seriously frustrated him.

He was excited to see his mother and sisters. They spoke often, but it had been months since he and Ash had time to visit them and t wasn't the same. Unfortunately, work had made that impossible given the whole Ricardo and then Pablo situation. But that was all taken care of now, and even though they were still hunting King, he doubted that would happen quickly. So, in the meantime, his family was going to spend two whole weeks with them prepping for the wedding. He hadn't been so sure it was a good idea, but Ash insisted. She loved having his family over, especially his mother. He assumed it was because she missed her own mother and his had been more than happy to take over the role.

He pulled into his driveway and, not seeing his mother's vehicle, realized he still had a few minutes to get changed before they would arrive. He found Ash in the kitchen and, with her back to him, he wrapped his arms around her and placed kisses along her neck.

"I was beginning to wonder if you would get here before your family. I take it the client was giving you a hard time?" She snuggled back into his arms.

"You could say that," he laughed. "But enough work talk. Let me get changed. I can only imagine what Ari and Jewels have been up to, and I prefer not to be in a stuffy suit when they tell me about their shenanigans."

He kissed her temple before rushing upstairs. While he loved his sisters dearly, they were both several years younger and made an art out of causing trouble. Nothing dangerous, but just enough to make him worry. He would prefer if they both settled down and took nice boring jobs, rather than constantly traveling or job-hopping.

He knew the moment his family arrived; his house was no longer quiet and he could hear the laughter of four extremely excited women downstairs. Most men would probably dread the onslaught, but he absolutely loved it. Not once growing up did he regret living in a house full of women, and he had the added benefit of knowing how happy it made Ash. And really, that was his only mission in life at this point.

He'd barely gotten to the bottom of the steps before Jeweliana was throwing herself into his arms. She was the youngest of the three of them, and since their father had left just a couple of months before she was born, they had all rallied around her growing up, giving her extra love and probably spoiling her just a little too much. Which was probably why his youngest sister felt the need to be so damn fiercely independent. It was no secret that she didn't want to be coddled and preferred to be as adventurous as possible.

"Hey, big brother! What are the chances I can convince you to let me go over to the barn while we are here and blow some shit up?" Jewels smiled sweetly up at him.

That was the other problem. His sister had tagged along with everything he had done, much to their mother's dismay, so not only did she have one child who loved danger, but another one as well. Jewels asked the same question any time she visited, and no matter how much he promised himself he wouldn't encourage her tomboyish behavior, he always caved to her wishes. He had no one to blame for her obsession but himself.

"We shall see," he started. "Wes has been grumpy and I'm not sure what plans Mama and Ash have."

"Your boss is always grumpy," Jewels laughed. "And you know Ash never says no."

His sister batted her eyelashes at him. Some guy was going to be in trouble one day. His sister looked innocent, but that's exactly where it stopped. With her looks. It took all of five minutes for a person to realize his baby sister used those looks to get what she wanted, but by that time, the poor person was already so far gone that they had no choice but to follow through on whatever they had promised.

"Maybe," he chuckled. "That's the best you're getting me to commit to." He shook his head when Jewels nearly gave him a huff and a roll of the eyes before rushing back to the kitchen. If he had to guess, his sister was already scheming how to make sure Ash agreed with her plan.

In the kitchen, he found everyone sitting around the small dining table.

"There's my boy! Did your sister harass you before you even got downstairs?" His mother's knowing smirk said it all.

"Did you expect anything less?" he laughed. "Hello, Mama." He dropped a kiss on her head, as well as both of his sisters', before pulling up a seat next to Ash. His fiancée snuggled up to him the moment he sat down.

"Ash was just about to discuss some of the plans she already has in place for the wedding," his mother told him.

They spent the next couple of hours going over the details. There wasn't much for him to do other than show up. He and the guys had already gotten fitted for their tuxes. Despite the casual feel, they would wear them for the ceremony and then change immediately into more casual attire. The women were going to Charlotte's the next day to try on the dresses, and Ash had already assigned all of the other tasks, so with only two weeks away, everything was ready to go. Well, except for the honeymoon. He still needed to finalize some of those details. He wanted it to be a surprise, so he couldn't ask Ash for her opinion.

Chapter 11

S he looked at herself in the mirror as Charlotte continued to make adjustments to her dress. This was her final fitting before the wedding and she absolutely loved the simple sweetheart A-line with just a small train. It was everything she envisioned. Ash had never thought about her wedding, but once she realized Bentley was her forever, she always pictured herself walking down the aisle in the exact dress she was wearing now. It was a good thing Charlotte had been able to take that vision and turn it into a reality.

"I wish I could travel more," Jewels said, redirecting her focus. "I would love to see and help people from undernourished areas."

Bentley's youngest sister was always talking about trying something new. In the two years that Ash had known her, Jewels has had at least a dozen different jobs. Some were mundane and others allowed her to travel and see new places. Her soon-to-be sister-in-law rarely stayed more than a month or two in any one place, and she always went back to Alabama, her home base. Jewels called herself a secret homebody whenever Ash asked her about it.

"If you're serious about wanting to help people, you could always come work for me at the halfway house. Or possibly travel to Mexico with me when Bravo Team shuts down another stable," Trista announced from where she was sitting across the room.

"Wait, what halfway house and what do you mean shuts down a stable?"

Ash knew Bentley didn't always tell his family about the type of assignments he was sent on. They knew about the security gigs and that he traveled occasionally, but she was pretty sure he never told them about Bravo Team.

"I started a halfway house a few months back for women who are transitioning back from being rescued from human trafficking," Trista answered matter-of-factly. "I give them a place to live, as well as help finding jobs or learning a new trade. Pretty much anything they want or need to learn to help them feel comfortable." Her best friend didn't brag, she simply stated.

"And who's Bravo Team?" Jewels appeared to be seriously considering Trista's offer and analyzing what was being said. She wasn't sure how Bentley would feel knowing that they were telling his baby sister more about his job and the darker sides of it.

"Wes's other team. They are mostly down in Mexico rescuing the women and then they send them to me," Trista explained further.

"And they let you go to Mexico with them?"

Jewels's new comment had Ash snorting, something Trista clearly didn't appreciate considering the dagger-like look she was getting from her best friend.

"Not exactly, but I keep trying," Trista started explaining. "I want to be there firsthand but trying to convince Wes and his asshole team leader to let me go is proving to be more of a challenge than I expected."

That was an understatement, and it didn't go unnoticed that Trista used the term "asshole team leader" rather than Falcon's real name. Actually, now that she thought about it, she wasn't sure what his real name was. Everyone always called him Falcon, and she never thought to ask Bentley what it was. She could ask her best friend, but she doubted Trista knew it either, and even if she did, she didn't seem much in the mood to talk about him.

"I might just take you up on that offer," Jewels answered, as both her mother and sister groaned. Neither had commented throughout the exchange, but from the look Holly was giving her daughter, it didn't take a rocket scientist to figure out that she wasn't exactly thrilled with her youngest daughter's new adventure.

"Finished." The conversation between Trista and Jewels had distracted her from what Charlotte was doing and, in that time, Charlotte had finished with the few alterations she needed to make.

"It's perfect," she breathed out. Trista, Ari, Holly, and Jewels all echoed their agreements.

"Come on, let's go check out what else I have." Charlotte wasn't custom-designing everyone else's dresses, but she had plenty of options already created that Holly, Ari, and Jewels could pick from. Three hours and several dozen dresses later, each of them had found a dress that they loved, and Charlotte had promised to have alterations done in plenty of time before the wedding. Her friend truly was a miracle worker.

"What are the plans for the rest of the day?" Trista asked.

"Heading over to Wes's place to see if there's anything else I want to add," she chuckled as both Charlotte and Trista groaned. Every single part of Wes's outdoor oasis had been installed because of her. It got to the point where she rarely even asked Wes his opinion. She just sent him her ideas, and most of the time, he ignored her, but bitched endlessly after those additions were added. It was their own little game. One she secretly felt like Wes loved to play.

"One day that man is going to find himself a woman and you're not going to get such free rein anymore," Charlotte chuckled.

"I would welcome him finding a woman, and besides, I'm pretty sure that any woman he finds is going to love his backyard. Who doesn't want their own beautiful outdoor oasis?" Everyone agreed in one way or another.

"I'm going to see if my brother will take me up on the offer to play with some of his new toys at work," Jewels added.

"A.K.A. you're going to just show up and beg until either Bentley or one of his teammates takes you out." She shook her head at Jewels's big grin.

"Exactly, and since you're headed that way anyway, you might as well just drop me off. There's no way Bentley will get upset if he sees you first." Jewels was purposely buttering her up, and it was working. Bentley wasn't the only one who would be happy. She loved when she got the chance to drop in and see him.

"All right, you win. I'll drop you off on the way through."

Rolling her eyes at Jewels's lame attempt to act surprised that she had gotten her way, Ash said her goodbyes to her friends with promises to meet up over the next few days for something other than wedding planning. It had been a while since she had time to just relax with Trista, and since Monica would be flying down in two days, it would give them a chance to all hang out and have some fun.

Chapter 12

Jewels was acting strange. Ever since she went with Ash for her fitting, she had been avoiding any of his questions. She had stopped by the barn that day and he had shown her some of the new equipment Wes had added, but every time he even mentioned her working or what she planned to do next, she would conveniently change the subject or avoid the topic altogether. Which, in itself, told him that whatever she had planned, there was a good chance he wouldn't like it. Of course, he would support anything she did. He always did. No matter how many heart attacks it gave him in the process.

But that would have to wait until another time. He was scheduled to meet Arlo, and he was running late. Scanning his way through the barn, he found his team leader waiting for him in the situation room, his laptop open in front of him. Since they had hired on Ray, their team leader wasn't tied down to electronics as much as he used to be. He could swear that Arlo missed it, though.

"That soon-to-be wife of yours keeping you busy?" Arlo didn't even turn around when he asked.

"More like a crazy baby sister who is probably up to no good," he huffed.

"Jewels putting you through the wringer?"

He sighed before answering. "I'm not sure. It's more like a gut feeling, but shy of cornering her, I probably won't get an answer."

"I would say, then, just corner her, but from what you've told me, that won't do any good except having her digging her heels in more," Arlo answered seriously. "Better to just keep a close eye and scoop in for the rescue if need be."

His best friend was probably right. As much as he wanted to believe that he could intimidate the answer out of his baby sister, he knew her better than that. She was known for being the most stubborn one of the family, and she had earned that reputation for good reason.

"But enough about Jewels," Bentley started. "How is Operation Honeymoon going?"

He rubbed his hands together with excitement. After the hiccups he and Ash faced in Paris the first time, he decided that for their honeymoon, he was going to take her back. Except this time, it would be more like a European tour.

He had convinced Ash to take two weeks away with him. Her new assistant, with the help of Leslie, would keep things running. His future wife only had one party during that time and everything was in order for it. At least, that's what Ash kept telling him, but he had a feeling that she would be checking in anyway. The woman couldn't help it and he could never get mad at her for wanting to make sure her dream business was in good hands.

"I've scheduled you a private plane, so there won't be any delays or emergency landings," Arlo explained. "The rest of what you requested is set and ready to go."

"You know, if this whole 'team leader' thing doesn't work out," he laughed, "you have a shot as a travel agent."

He could have done the work on his own, but he didn't want Ash to know what he was planning, and when he told Leah and Arlo about his dilemma, Leah had offered to help get the information and set everything up. He had no idea how she did it, but he owed his best friend's wife big-time.

"Fuck you, asshole. Leah did all the work. Except for the private plane. That was all me. I happen to know a few of Wes's contacts who didn't mind lending their pilots," Arlo huffed.

"Speaking of our fearless leader, where is he and what is with the attitude lately?"

"I'm not sure." Arlo frowned. "I thought for sure after we took out Pablo he would be back to his old self, but now I'm beginning to think it's something else besides work. I know King's lack of an identity is really getting to him, but it feels like something else is going on."

"Ash thinks it has to do with a woman, but I quickly shut that idea down. I can't see a woman getting under his skin like this. And if it is a woman, heaven help her because taming our boss is no easy feat."

"Who said anything about taming?" Arlo barked out a laugh. "You don't really think that's what the women do to us?"

"I know damn well it's exactly what they do to us, and so do you." He laughed right along with his friend. "Leah practically has you wrapped around her finger, and she's the only one who gets the nice side of you. Same thing with the rest of us."

"You're right. The best thing that ever happened to me was finding my angel. I would have preferred better circumstances, but I wouldn't change having her in my life," Arlo answered him thoughtfully.

He could just imagine what his friend was remembering. Leah had been shot when she escaped from her ex-husband and then, months later, kidnapped and held hostage for weeks while they learned that her ex-husband was actually a serial killer. Arlo had every reason to be protective of his wife. He had almost lost her. All of his teammates had similar stories. Their relationships were forged during painful times, and because of it, they came out stronger than ever.

"I better get going before my sisters convince Ash to cause even more trouble. Jewels is up to something and my soon-to-be wife will be the first one to cheer her on."

"I don't envy you, brother. Good luck with that."

He could still hear Arlo's laughter as he walked down the hall. Luck is exactly what he would need. He loved his youngest sister, but once she got something into her head, there was no changing her mind. So whatever hairbrained scheme she had come up with, he was sure she would follow it through. He just hoped whatever it was, she wouldn't get into trouble. But he highly doubted it. Trouble was Jeweliana's middle name.

Chapter 13

Today was finally the day. She was just minutes away from walking downstairs and saying *I do* to the love of her life. "I'm going to cry. You look so beautiful." Monica's whimsical voice from her spot on the chaise lounge floated around her.

"Don't you dare start crying because if you do, then I will and then Ash will, and before you know it, we are all going to be walking down the aisle looking like a bunch of damn raccoons," Trista huffed with a hand on her hip. The rant did exactly what Trista wanted; they were all laughing too hard to start crying.

She glanced at her two best friends through the mirror. They had been through so many ups and downs over the years. She and Trista had gone through high school together, but out of their group of eight, only the two of them still spoke. And then they brought Monica into the fold when she met her during college. It only took one time of hanging out for Trista and Monica to hit it off. Not that she was surprised by that. Trista seemed to have a way of making friends. Everyone loved her blunt and bubbly attitude. Everyone except Falcon, that is.

Her phone alarm beeped from its spot next to Monica on the chaise lounge. That was her two-minute warning that she needed to start making her way downstairs. Checking herself one last time in the mirror, she turned toward her best friends. "Let's get this show on the road."

There were no pre-wedding jitters. She had been prepared to start the ceremony the moment she had been done getting ready. She only set the alarm because she had been driving Monica and Trista crazy by looking at it every thirty seconds to see if the time had come. She hadn't known how long an hour could feel until today.

Looking down the stairs, she found her father waiting to escort her. Despite all their differences, he was smiling up at her. He may have questioned every decision she had made but, just that morning, he had come to apologize to her. He admitted to not handling things very well. Like every father, he just wanted what was best, but it wasn't until he saw how happy Bentley really made her that he finally realized what she already knew. She and Bentley had a rare love. One that would last the tests of time. Then he had the audacity to tell her that he wanted grandchildren. Lots of them and as soon as possible. She had been tempted to strangle him for an all-new reason, but in the end, she couldn't. She wanted kids just as much as he wanted grandchildren.

She held her father's gaze as she descended the stairs, stopping only to take his outstretched arm. "You look beautiful. Your mother would be so proud of you," he whispered.

She tried to blink back the tears. Contrary to what Trista said, she knew the woman who did their makeup had used a waterproof mascara, but that didn't mean she wanted to tempt fate and ruin her face before Bentley had the chance to see her.

With one more deep breath to completely eliminate all the tears, she stepped out through the glass doors and got her first look at Bentley. He was, of course, dashingly handsome in his tuxedo, and it reminded her of the first gala they attended together. At the time, he had been her bodyguard, but he had already been on his way to being so much more. She should probably thank her father's old business partner. If it wasn't for him, she would never have met Bentley.

She wanted to hike up her dress and run straight into Bentley's arms, but she stopped the urge. Barely. Instead, she walked in tune to the wedding march. Each step took her closer and closer to her future. After what felt like forever, she was finally standing in front of the man she loved with all her heart.

She tuned out the officiant as her hand was placed from her father's arm to Bentley's. She barely even felt the kiss her father placed on her cheek. All she could focus on was the bright smile on Bentley's face and how his piercing blue eyes never left hers. Later, if she was asked to remember what was said around her, she could honestly say the entire ceremony passed by in a dream. Until Bentley kissed her. Then the world melted away, and it was just the two of them.

She was still floating on cloud nine an hour later when she and Bentley danced together on the makeshift dance floor. Bentley had changed into a pair of cargo shorts and a dress shirt. Fortunately for her, the dress Charlotte designed wasn't heavy, so she didn't mind staying in it. And she had been able to pin up the small train.

"Are you happy, Mrs. Grey?" She loved the sound of that. Just as much as she loved hearing his husky voice whispering in her ear as they glided around.

"Very," she replied. "And are you?"

"More than anything else. I love you, Ash. For better or worse and everything in between. I promise to always make sure you're happy."

The smile that spread across her face couldn't be missed by anyone in attendance. If they didn't already know how happy the newly married couple was, they had only to look at the love pouring out of each of them. A love that would stand the test of time.

Epilogue

Ash sat around the bonfire and looked at the women of Charlie Team. Leah sat next to her with Sophie in her lap, half asleep. Leslie was on the other side of Leah, rubbing her pregnant belly in circles. In typical Zack fashion, he had announced when they all gathered together at his place that he and Leslie had finally chosen a name. Little Matthew Zackary Lynch wasn't even born yet and already the little guy was so loved. Zack and Leslie were going to make great parents.

"What do you think the guys are talking about over there?" She tilted her head towards where the guys were sitting in a similar position around another fire in Leslie's yard. The wedding was yesterday, and they had decided to get together tonight as a group before she and Bentley left on their honeymoon. Her husband wanted the location to be a surprise, so she had no idea where they were going or for how long. *Husband. I still can't believe how that sounds.*

"Probably discussing what they are going to blow up next when you guys get back, since they were deprived of a bachelor party." Jaime snorted.

The guys had grumbled when Bentley explained that they planned not to wait long and wanted a small, intimate wedding. They felt they were being robbed of throwing Bentley one hell of a rager, according to Zack. Which, in their terms, meant they planned to blow up as much stuff as they could before Wes yelled at them. Speaking of Wes, she was getting concerned about the man. His normal gruff self was at an all-time high. She had tried asking him about it, but to no avail. He shut her down quickly with a not-so-subtle *mind your own damn business* remark.

"More like betting which one of us they will knock up next," Leah chuckled. Four heads whipped in Leah's direction. Raising the one hand that wasn't supporting her daughter, Leah added, "Not me. Arlo and I already discussed we want to wait until I get the business settled before trying again."

"Ugh, Zack's already talking about having more and I haven't even pushed this little guy out yet," Leslie groaned.

She hadn't had the chance to talk to Bentley yet, but she wanted to start trying sooner rather than later. Her business was starting to take off, so she finally felt like she could handle both. Especially since Trista had come through and helped her hire an assistant. Once she got back from her honeymoon, she was going to add another employee or two, so there was no reason they needed to wait.

"Well, Kade is very much aware that I'm not even close to being ready to have kids yet, so count me out."

Missy's soft groan caught all of their attention. "They might have their answer sooner than you think."

"Wait, what?!" Ash nearly lunged off her seat but stopped herself when both Missy and Leah gave her a scowl. Leah would be pissed to all hell if she accidentally woke up Sophie. The poor little girl hadn't been sleeping well the past few nights. "Are you saying what I think you're saying?" Ash whispered loudly.

Missy's face was the shade of a tomato when she nodded. "I took a test this morning but wanted to wait until we were alone to tell him. I'm not sure how Kyle is going to feel about it. We haven't exactly discussed the topic yet. We are still in the process of finalizing the adoptions."

Now that they were positive both Ella and Kallie didn't have any more surprise family members looking for them, Bentley had explained that Kyle was eager to get the adoption completed. From what her husband had said, it wouldn't be much longer. She knew for a fact those two little girls would be thrilled to be big sisters. They loved Sophie and weren't shy about telling Leslie that they couldn't wait for Matthew to be born.

"Well, congratulations," she started. "And I think he will be thrilled. But beware, he might demand you get married at once. He's a bit overprotective of you three. Add a fourth and he won't wait long to drag you down the aisle."

That brought a chuckle to Missy's lips, as well as the rest of them. It was no secret each of the guys was a bit obsessive and more than a tad overprotective. Watching first Arlo and then Zack hover over their pregnant wives, she could pretty much guess Kyle wouldn't be any different.

More congratulations were thrown around, and by the time everyone assured Missy that Kyle would be thrilled, her new friend was smiling from ear to ear. The nerves that were written all over her face just moments earlier had vanished into thin air.

Bentley looked over at his wife. *My wife. I'll never get tired of saying that.* Yesterday was by far the best day of his life. He had thought it was a crazy idea to throw together a wedding so quickly, but he should never have underestimated Ash. As usual, she and the rest of the women rallied together and gave them one hell of an incredible day.

"Where's the boss tonight?" Kade asked. "I expected him to be here."

"Said he was busy and would catch up with us later." Zack shrugged. "Maybe he was mad we weren't meeting at his place for once."

Bentley doubted that was the case. When Leslie had mentioned that she wasn't feeling the best, they all quickly agreed to move their little post-wedding hangout to Zack's backyard. It was almost a mirror image of Wes's anyway, minus the lake. Zack insisted he needed a backyard oasis as well, and that's exactly what he designed. One that had two separate firepits where the men and women could gather together in their own groups just like they were doing now.

"I'm giving him a couple of days before I knock some sense into him," Arlo grumbled.

They all had noticed the bad attitude lately. Wes was grumpier than normal and it made no sense. They had successfully taken care of Pablo and were still actively looking for King. They had at least one win in their corner, so there was no reason for the hostility that had been pouring off their boss lately.

"Maybe he just needs to get laid," Kade joked.

"Pretty sure I would love to see his reaction when you suggest that," he snickered. "It just might be worth seeing him haul off and slug you for a comment like that."

"I'd take one for the team." Kade took a swig of his beer.

"You're awfully quiet tonight." Bentley gestured towards Kyle. "Everything good with the girls?"

"Yeah, they are great," Kyle quickly replied. "The adoption is almost finalized, so soon we won't have to worry about any other family members. Wes has expedited the process, so that's good."

"Then why the solemn face?" Zack threw out.

Kyle blew out a breath before answering in a low voice. "I'm pretty sure Missy took a pregnancy test this morning, but she hasn't mentioned anything, and she's been super jumpy all day." His teammate's face looked worried.

"Maybe's she worried how you will feel about it if she is," Arlo spoke up first. "I remember when Leah told me she was nervous because it was a surprise. I'm guessing the two of you haven't discussed it?"

Kyle ran his hands through his short hair. "No, we haven't, but only because we were focused on the adoptions. But I certainly planned on talking about it. That and marriage."

"So, would you be happy if she was?" Zack asked.

"Of course I would be!" Kyle exclaimed.

"Then make sure tonight, when you go home, she knows that." Arlo shrugged. "We need more kids in this group, anyway.

Bentley and Kade need to do their part as well." Their team leader chuckled at his declaration.

"Oh, I firmly plan on working on that during the honeymoon," Bentley laughed. "No worries here."

"Yeah, I have no plans on starting that anytime soon, so I'll just keep playing the cool uncle," Kade added, causing a round of laughter. Their teammate seemed so sure, which was fine. The rest of them could pick up the slack in the meantime.

"When did things change so much?" Zack asked thoughtfully. "Two years ago we would be hanging out like this and talking about what assignments we had coming up or reminiscing over old ones. Now it's baby talk."

Zack wasn't wrong. So much had changed in that time and it all started with one job. One kidnapping that led Bentley to the love of his life and, like a domino effect, the rest of his teammates fell after him. All five had finally found the women that complemented them in the best ways possible. Single life wasn't for them anymore. They would leave that to Wes and Bravo Team.

Where to find me:

Interested in staying in touch?
I love connecting with my readers.
For sneak peeks, teasers, and a fun community
please join Elizabella's Ladies Reader Group
or follow me on Instagram, TikTok, Goodreads, and Bookbub.

Acknowledgments

To my readers! Without you none of this would be possible. Thank you to each person who has taken a chance on a new author! I appreciate your support more than you will ever know. Thank you so much!□

Also By Elizabella Baker

Fighting for Charlotte

Burning for Chloe

Caring for Lucy

Bravo Team Series:

Protecting Ember

Chasing Trista

Stand-Alone:

Westley